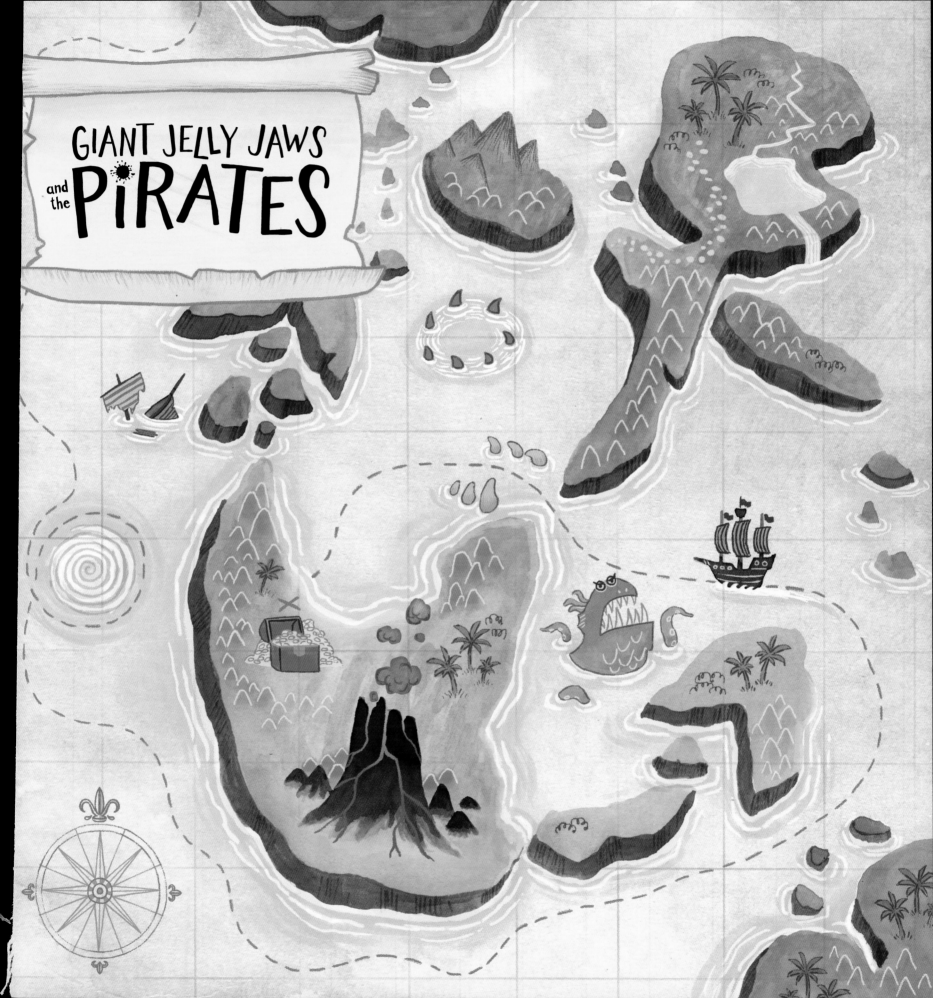

For Chloe, Jacob,
Alex and Sofia~H. B.

For Poppy~B. M.

First published in paperback in Great Britain by HarperCollins Children's Books in 2016
First published in hardback in 2016

10 9 8 7 6 5 4 3 2 1

ISBN: 978-0-00-816725-7

HarperCollins Children's Books is a division of HarperCollins Publishers Ltd.

Text copyright © Helen Baugh 2016
Illustrations copyright © HarperCollins Publishers Ltd 2016

Visit our website at: www.harpercollins.co.uk

Printed in China

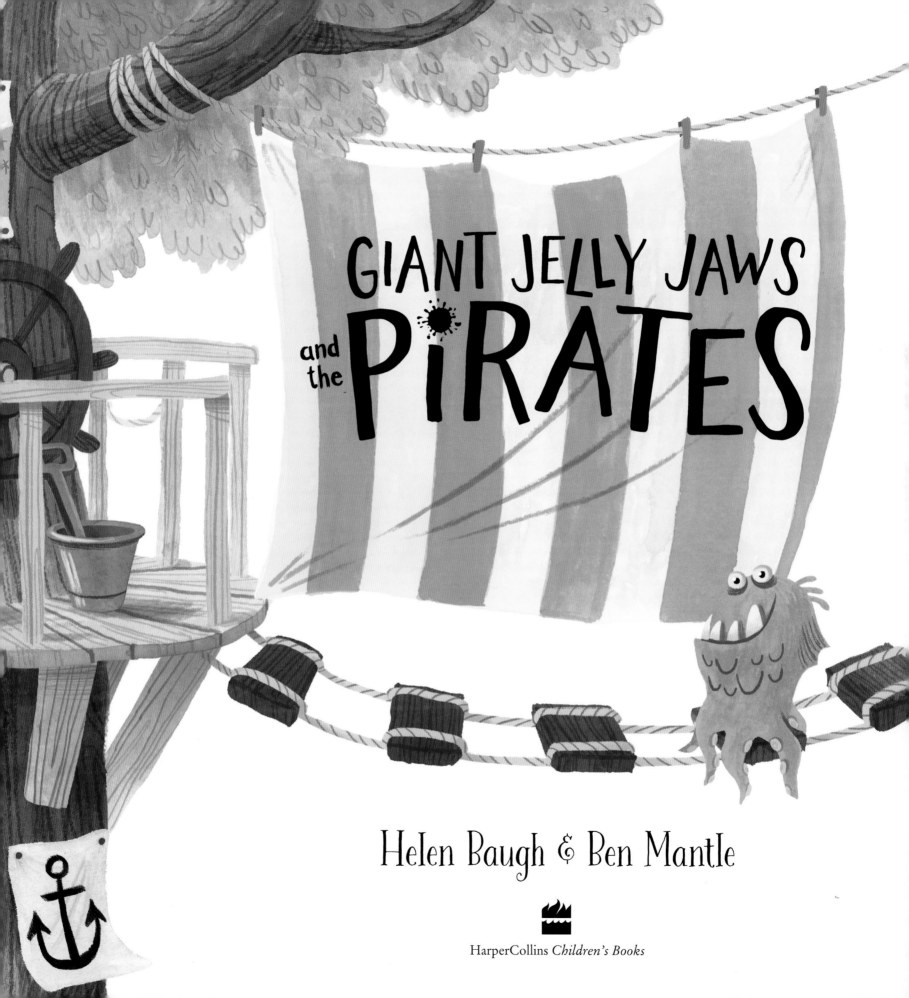

GIANT JELLY JAWS and the PIRATES

Helen Baugh & Ben Mantle

HarperCollins *Children's Books*

Since he was a little boy,
of two or maybe three,
Jake had longed to sail away
with pirates out to sea.

And now at last
the day had come
for Jake to say, "Ahoy!"
He was going to join
a pirate crew
and be their cabin boy.

"Hurry up, landlubber!"
Snot-Nose Ned cried. "Don't delay!
This treasure map will make us rich.
A-harrr! Anchors away!"

The pirates on the ship
were all too fierce to live indoors.
Fish~Breath Fred, the captain,
kept live lobsters in his drawers!

And as Jake soon discovered, they were quite revolting, too.
Each man had rotten teeth and fleas and smelled of fish gut stew. (Ewww!)

Although Jake tried to fit in
once the ship was out at sea,

his hands were soft...

he smelled of soap...

he cried when he
skinned his knee.

He didn't have the courage
to climb up to the crow's nest.

He didn't have the heart to catch
the rats who were a pest.

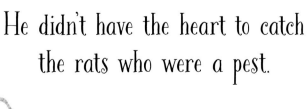

Then Toot-Pants Pete found out
that Jake had never had a fight~

and even worse he still slept
with his teddy bear at night!

Captain Fish-Breath Fred in fury
stamped and stomped and cursed.
"Of all the cabin boys we've ever had,
ye be the worst!"

Then one night Jake asked, "Please tell me: who's your figurehead?"
"It's Giant Jelly Jaws~to scare our foes," Long~John Jim said.

The crew drank lots of pirate pop and burped and shared their tales,
of the grisly, gruesome sea monster the size of seven whales.

"It stings just like a jellyfish and bites just like a shark!"

"It can smell you from ten miles away and see you in the dark!"

"It sucks in massive gulps of air and makes the loudest burps!"

"It can swallow pirate ships like this down whole in just two slurps!"

The next day Butt~Beard Bob
woke all the pirates with a yell.
He'd seen another Jolly Roger
high above the swell!

"Shake a leg, me hearties!
I've got a nasty hunch
that a scurvy bunch of bilge rats
wants to have our **brains for brunch!**"

The whole crew jumped straight to it,
getting ready for a fight...

except for Jake, who hid behind some kegs of pop in fright.

The other pirates soon arrived
and caused a huge uproar.
"Give up your treasure map, you grubs,
or be prepared for war!"

Captain Fish~Breath Fred stood firm
and snorted in disgust.
"This treasure map is OURS!
So brace your britches:
fight we must!"

Both sides fought hard and dirty,
using brawn and brain and muscle…

...but in the end the other team of pirates won the tussle.

Shiver me timbers, mateys!
The situation stank!
Without some kind of miracle,
the gang would walk the plank!

Still down behind the kegs of pop, Jake looked on in dismay.
How ever was he going to make things right and save the day?

But then Jake saw the answer,
in a keg of pirate pop.

He opened up the barrel,
and then drank down every drop!

In a matter of mere moments
his small belly grew quite round,

then down from deep within it
came a rumbly sort of sound.

The bubbles rose up to his nose
and tickled like a feather,

but Jake sniffed hard to snort them down
and pursed his lips together.

When the time was right at last,
Jake didn't have a doubt:
he opened up his mouth...

and let a monster

B-U-R-R-

Every single pirate's blood ran ice~cold at the sound.
A noise like that meant Giant Jelly Jaws must be around!
"Abandon ship!" the captain of the rogue pirates decreed.

Then off they sailed in mortal fear
and panic at full speed.

Captain Fish-Breath Fred and crew
thought they were surely doomed;
that all they could do now was wait
in dread to be consumed.

But then they heard
Jake's little voice cry,

"Shipmates! Don't you see?
Giant Jelly Jaws was not the burper …

it was me!"

The pirates were astounded.
The boy had saved them all!

Who would have thought a burp so BIG
could come from one so small?!

Much manly hugging later
(and a secret tear or two),
the pirates checked their map once more
and sailed off through the blue.

When they reached the island,
Booger~Bill soon found the spot:

the "X" marked on their map
where they should dig for the jackpot.

The pirates were so happy that their
quest was at an end!

They shared a tasty fish stick feast
and praised their new~found friend...

"Burp~Boy Jake, you saved us all
and helped us find this chest.
Of all the cabin boys we've ever had,
ye be the BEST!"